BIGGEST NAMES IN SPORTS

JUSTIN HERBERT

FOOTBALL STAR

by Alex Monnig

FOCUS READERS®
NAVIGATOR

WWW.FOCUSREADERS.COM

Focus Readers is distributed by North Star Editions:
sales@northstareditions.com | 888-417-0195

Produced for Focus Readers by Red Line Editorial.

Photographs ©: Ben Liebenberg/LIEBB/AP Images, cover, 1, 25; Peter Joneleit/AP Images, 4–5, 9; Kyusung Gong/AP Images, 7; Brian Murphy/Icon Sportswire/SPTSW/AP Images, 10–11, 15, 18; Steve Conner/Icon Sportswire/SPTSW/AP Images, 13; Larry C. Lawson/Cal Sport Media/ZUMA Wire/AP Images, 16–17; Mark J. Terrill/AP Images, 21; Jae C. Hong/AP Images, 22–23; Ric Tapia/TAPIR/AP Images, 27; Red Line Editorial, 29

Library of Congress Cataloging-in-Publication Data
Names: Monnig, Alex, author.
Title: Justin Herbert : football star / by Alex Monnig.
Description: Lake Elmo, MN : Focus Readers, [2023] | Series: Biggest names in sports ; Set 7 | Includes index. | Audience: Grades 4-6
Identifiers: LCCN 2022016630 (print) | LCCN 2022016631 (ebook) | ISBN 9781637392560 (Hardcover) | ISBN 9781637393086 (Paperback) | ISBN 9781637394090 (PDF) | ISBN 9781637393604 (eBook)
Subjects: LCSH: Herbert, Justin, 1998---Juvenile literature. | Quarterbacks (Football)--United States--Biography--Juvenile literature. | Football players--United States--Biography--Juvenile literature. | Oregon Ducks (Football team)--History--Juvenile literature. | Football--California--Los Angeles--Juvenile literature.
Classification: LCC GV939.H465 M66 2023 (print) | LCC GV939.H465 (ebook) | DDC 796.33092 [B]--dc23/eng/20220509
LC record available at https://lccn.loc.gov/2022016630
LC ebook record available at https://lccn.loc.gov/2022016631

Printed in the United States of America
Mankato, MN
082022

ABOUT THE AUTHOR

Alex Monnig is a freelance writer from St. Louis, Missouri. Since graduating from the University of Missouri, Alex has covered sporting events around the world, including the Olympic Games, Rugby World Cup, Commonwealth Games, and more. He now lives in Sydney, Australia.

TABLE OF CONTENTS

CHARGERS
NFL
10
NFL

CHAPTER 1

A SURPRISING START

Los Angeles Chargers quarterback Justin Herbert warmed up on the sidelines. It was Week 2 of the 2020 National Football League (NFL) season. The Chargers were about to play the Kansas City Chiefs. Shortly before kickoff, Chargers head coach Anthony Lynn walked up to Herbert. He said

Justin Herbert warms up before a 2020 game against the Kansas City Chiefs.

Herbert would be the **starter**. The **rookie** was stunned. Herbert had expected to be the **backup**. But the team's starting quarterback couldn't play because of an injury. Now Herbert was starting against the NFL's defending champions.

After the kickoff, the Chargers offense took the field. Herbert missed his first pass attempt. On the next play, Herbert prepared to pass again. He scanned the Chiefs defense. He told his offensive linemen where to block. Then he took the snap. Five Chiefs defenders rushed him. Herbert looked to his left. The receiver was covered. He turned to his right and tossed the ball to running back Joshua

Herbert reads the defense before taking a snap.

Kelley. Kelley sprinted down the field for a 35-yard pickup.

Herbert's throw wasn't difficult. Even so, reading the defense and making a good decision was impressive. After all, Herbert was a rookie and a backup.

Soon, the Chargers faced third down. Herbert took the snap from Kansas City's 20-yard line. Three Chiefs defenders were about to tackle him. Herbert shuffled backward. Then he lofted a pass to the left for a 16-yard completion.

That brought the Chargers to the 4-yard line. Herbert went under center and took the snap. He curled to his right. All of his receivers were covered. So, Herbert faked a throw. Then he sprinted into the corner of the endzone. Herbert's teammates ran over to celebrate with him. He had scored on his first drive as a pro!

Herbert went on to throw for 311 yards in the game. He recorded one touchdown

Herbert celebrates after throwing the first touchdown pass of his NFL career.

pass and one interception. Unfortunately for Chargers fans, the Chiefs ended up winning 23–20. Still, Herbert's teammates loved the rookie's toughness and vision. In his surprise start, Herbert had shown he was ready for the big time.

NIKE
10

CHAPTER 2

HOMETOWN HERO

Justin Herbert was born on March 10, 1998, in Eugene, Oregon. Growing up, Justin loved football. Eugene is the home of the University of Oregon. Justin's grandfather sometimes took him to Ducks games. Justin also cheered for the NFL's Chargers, who were based in San Diego at the time.

Justin Herbert expected to be a backup during his freshman year at Oregon.

Justin played football at Sheldon High School. In his senior season, he threw and ran for a combined 47 touchdowns. He also led his team to a 10–2 record. The University of Oregon offered him a **scholarship**. He was going to be playing for his favorite team.

Herbert's first two seasons at Oregon had highs and lows. In 2016, he was a **freshman**. Herbert impressed the coaches with his dedication and ability. Many young players begin as backups. That's what Herbert expected, too. But Oregon struggled in the first part of the season. Coaches wanted to make a change. So, in the sixth game of the season, they

Herbert looks for a receiver during his first game as Oregon's starting quarterback.

made Herbert the starter. The Ducks were facing the fifth-ranked Washington Huskies. Not surprisingly, Oregon lost.

Herbert started the rest of the season. The team went 2–5 under his leadership. But the young quarterback showed off his skill. After the loss to Washington, Herbert tied a school record with six touchdown passes against the University of California. The following week, he tied a school record with 489 passing yards in a win over Arizona State.

Hopes were high for Herbert's sophomore season. The team started 3–1 and had a high-flying offense.

A STAR IN THE CLASSROOM

Justin Herbert shined as brightly in the classroom as he did on the field. He won several academic awards while studying general science with a focus in biology. Both his dad and grandfather were teachers. Herbert loved science as much as he loved football. He was even a tutor for other students.

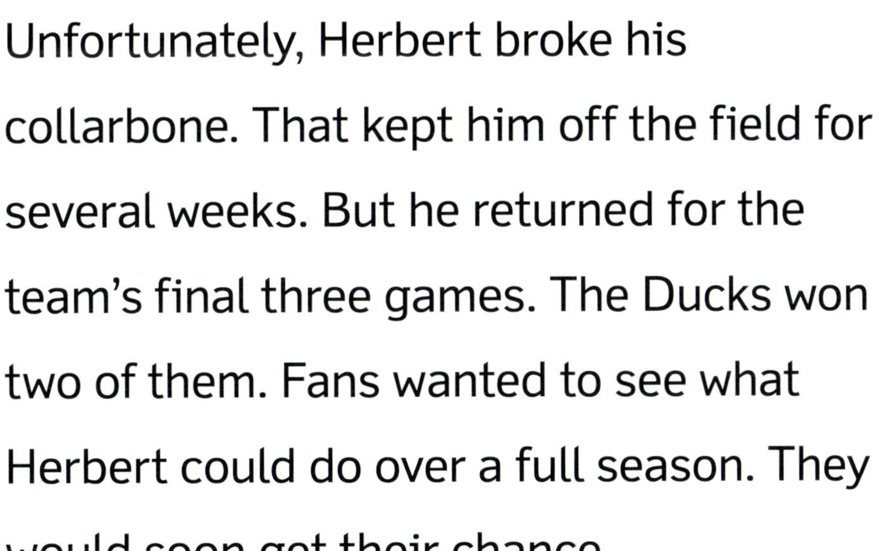

Herbert runs with the ball during a 2017 game against Southern Utah.

Unfortunately, Herbert broke his collarbone. That kept him off the field for several weeks. But he returned for the team's final three games. The Ducks won two of them. Fans wanted to see what Herbert could do over a full season. They would soon get their chance.

10

CHAPTER 3

TAKING OVER OREGON

College football fans had seen flashes of Justin Herbert's talent. Entering the 2018 season, many people thought he could win the **Heisman Trophy**. Herbert had no quarterbacks ahead of him. He also had no injuries that kept him from starting. Herbert didn't waste any time showing what he could do.

Herbert fires a pass during a 2018 game against Portland State.

Herbert leads the Oregon Ducks to victory over the Washington Huskies in 2018.

The Ducks started the season 5–1. That included an exciting overtime win over Washington. It was Herbert's first victory against Oregon's **rival**. The Ducks finished the season with a solid 9–4 record. Herbert's strong play was a big reason for their success.

During his junior season, Herbert topped 5,000 career passing yards. No Oregon quarterback had ever done it faster. Herbert's size and passing ability impressed many NFL **scouts**. So did his ability to run with the ball.

Many football experts thought Herbert would enter the NFL **Draft** after his junior season. Some experts even said he would be a first-round pick. That would mean getting paid millions of dollars. But Herbert surprised them. He returned for his fourth and final year with the Ducks.

Herbert was excited about the team. He also wanted to finish his degree.

Oregon fans were thrilled that he stayed. And in 2019, Herbert had his best season. The Ducks went 12–2. Herbert won his first Pac-12 Conference title. He also set career highs by passing for 3,471 yards and 32 touchdowns.

PREPARING FOR THE DRAFT

Herbert didn't have to go far to find people to train with before the NFL Draft. His brothers Mitchell and Patrick were also college football players. They all lived together. Five times a week leading up to the draft, the three brothers trained near their home in Eugene. The training helped Justin work on his skills before he practiced in front of NFL teams.

Herbert sprints for a touchdown against the Wisconsin Badgers during the Rose Bowl.

In his final game as a Duck, Herbert ran for three touchdowns. More importantly, he led Oregon to an exciting 28–27 victory in the Rose Bowl. Herbert left Oregon on a winning note. Now it was time to show what he could do in the NFL.

SoFi
10

CHAPTER 4

A BOLT OF EXCITEMENT

In the 2020 NFL Draft, the Los Angeles Chargers chose Justin Herbert sixth overall. Herbert had just spent four years playing for his favorite college team. Now he'd be playing for his favorite pro team.

Herbert expected to be a backup at first. That would give him time to learn from older players. But his surprise start

Herbert practices with the Chargers before the 2020 season.

against the Chiefs changed that. Herbert was leading a team again. And this time, it was at the highest level.

Herbert started the rest of the 2020 season. In his fifth game, he finally notched his first win. But after that, Los Angeles lost five of the next six games. That included a 45–0 blowout to the New

MAKING A DIFFERENCE

Justin Herbert has also made an impact off the field through his charity work. In 2018, he went to the African nation of Uganda to help build a sports court for kids. In 2021, he hosted the Justin Herbert Invitational golf tournament. It raised money for youth sports programs in the Eugene area.

Herbert earned his first victory as a starter against the Jacksonville Jaguars in Week 7 of the 2020 season.

England Patriots. Despite the bumpy start, Herbert didn't get discouraged.

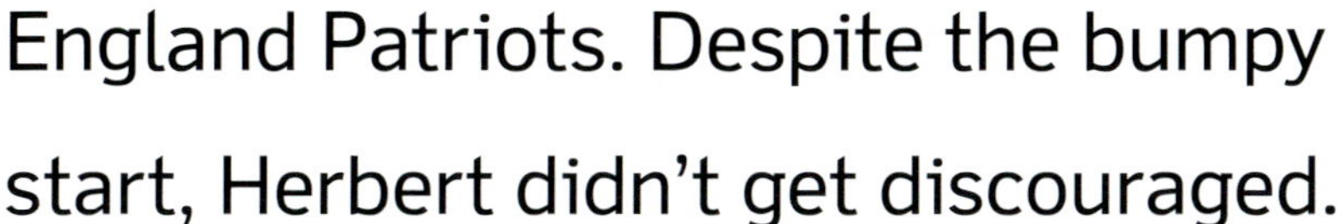

The Chargers turned a corner after the shutout. They won their final four games with Herbert leading the way. By the end of the season, Herbert had set rookie records with 31 passing touchdowns and 396 completions. Not surprisingly, he was named Offensive Rookie of the Year.

In 2021, Herbert was even better. That season, he tossed 38 touchdown passes. He also led the Chargers to five fourth-quarter comebacks. And he almost made it six. In the last game of the season, Los Angeles faced the Las Vegas Raiders. With less than nine minutes left, the Chargers trailed by 15 points. But Herbert stayed cool. He threw two touchdown passes to tie the game.

Unfortunately for Herbert, the Raiders ended up winning in overtime. That

Herbert competes against the Las Vegas Raiders in the final game of the 2021 season.

meant the Chargers missed the playoffs. Even so, Los Angeles fans had plenty to be excited about. With Herbert on the team, fans hoped there would be many more playoff chances in the future.

JUSTIN HERBERT

- Height: 6 feet 6 inches (198 cm)
- Weight: 237 pounds (108 kg)
- Birth date: March 10, 1998
- Birthplace: Eugene, Oregon
- High school: Sheldon High School (Eugene, Oregon)
- College: University of Oregon (Eugene, Oregon) (2016–19)
- NFL team: Los Angeles Chargers (2020–)
- Major awards: Pac-12 title (2019); William V. Campbell Trophy (2019); NFL Offensive Rookie of the Year (2020); Pro Bowl (2021)

Eugene
Los Angeles

FOCUS ON
JUSTIN HERBERT

Write your answers on a separate piece of paper.

1. Write a sentence that explains the main idea of Chapter 3.

2. Do you think Herbert should have gone to the NFL after his junior year? Why or why not?

3. Which team did the Chargers play during Herbert's first NFL start?

- **A.** Las Vegas Raiders
- **B.** Kansas City Chiefs
- **C.** New England Patriots

4. Why were Chargers fans happy with the 2021 season even though the team missed the playoffs?

- **A.** The Chargers planned to get a new quarterback to replace Herbert.
- **B.** The Chargers did worse than expected, but they would have a good draft pick the next year.
- **C.** The Chargers did better than expected, and Herbert had turned into a strong leader.

Answer key on page 32.

GLOSSARY

backup

A player who does not start the game.

draft

A system that allows teams to acquire new players coming into a league.

freshman

A first-year student.

Heisman Trophy

The award given to the best college football player each season.

rival

A team or player that has an intense and ongoing competition against another team or player.

rookie

A professional athlete in his or her first year.

scholarship

Money given to a student to pay for education expenses.

scouts

People whose jobs involve looking for talented young players.

starter

A player who participates in a game from its beginning.

TO LEARN MORE

BOOKS

Savage, Jeff. *Football Super Stats*. Minneapolis: Lerner Publications, 2018.

Whiting, Jim. *Los Angeles Chargers*. Mankato, MN: Creative Paperbacks, 2019.

York, Andy. *Ultimate College Football Road Trip*. Minneapolis: Abdo Publishing, 2019.

NOTE TO EDUCATORS

Visit **www.focusreaders.com** to find lesson plans, activities, links, and other resources related to this title.

INDEX

Answer Key: 1. Answers will vary; **2.** Answers will vary; **3.** B; **4.** C